Mop

I don't know what my plan was when I threw myself out the window.

I don't know if I even had a plan at all.

All that mattered was getting away from the people in that room.

So there I was: Thirty feet above the ground.

No way up.

No way down.

I was stuck...

MARK CRILLEY

HarperCollins *Children's Books*

春 ·BOOK ONE· SPRING

I'm coming down...

...when I'm *ready* to come down.

After a quick breakfast I headed off for school.

I don't know what it was...

...maybe just something in the air...

...but I had an incredible sense of well-being that morning.

Like I was ready to take on the world.

Ready, in fact...

But Miki, there was such a spaced-out look in your eyes.

You were practically begging for it.

A simple "snap out of it" would do nicely, thank you.

So who were you thinking about?

Yoshi? Sho? Tetsu? Masa?

You know, hard as it may be for you to believe, some of us...

...every once in a while...

...think about something other than guys.

It was Tetsu, wasn't it?

Tell me again why you're so obsessed with my love life.

Or lack thereof.

Look, you've got to give Tetsu a break. He's nuts about you. He's just too shy to ask you out.

Yumi, Tetsu is *far* beyond shy. Every time a girl makes eye contact with him he goes catatonic.

Okay, how about Yoshi? He's not shy.

Yoshi...

...is a sleazeball.

Dating him would be like putting on a pair of wet socks.

16

PATTA
PATTA
PATTA

...do us all a favor and pursue some excellent **breath mints**.

Stop it already!

Come on, we're gonna be late as it is.

So Yumi and I continued down the road to school...

Say, what about Kota-kun?

He **loves** fermented bean curd...

...and my senior year began in earnest.

22

As it turned out, Hiro Sakurai wouldn't join any club at our school. He just wasn't a club-joining kind of guy.

But we had no clue about that at the time.

Me, I was a member of the kyuudou club.

Later that day the club met for a few hours of practice.

Kyuudou requires a focused mind.

To do it right you've got to shut yourself off from the outside world...

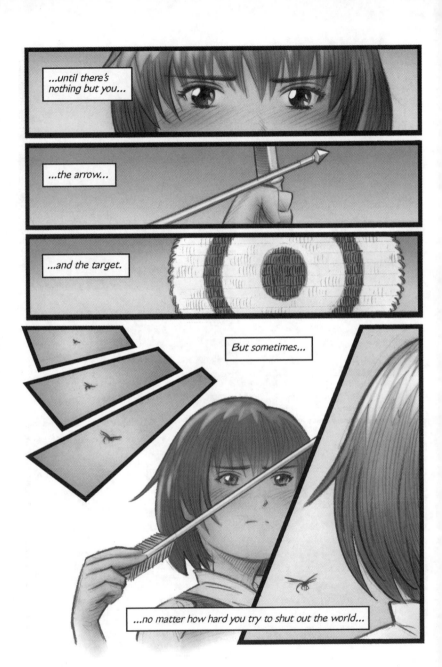

...until there's nothing but you...

...the arrow...

...and the target.

But sometimes...

...no matter how hard you try to shut out the world...

24

I never did find that arrow.

I found something, though.

Or rather...

...some**one**.

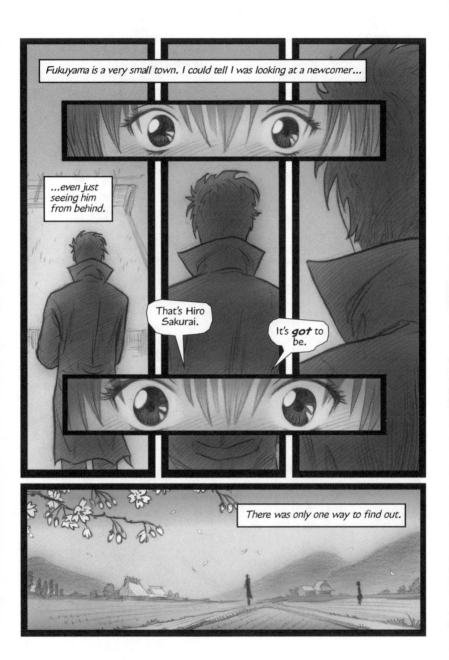

29

Excuse me, but aren't you...

He spun around and stared at me with eyes wide open.

There was an awkward pause.

A **very** awkward pause.

He thrust whatever he'd been holding into his trench coat and kept his lips shut tight.

The next morning Hiro Sakurai made his big debut at Fukuyama High.

One by one, groups of students tried to befriend him, and they all came back with the same verdict...

He was a cold fish, through and through.

I had never seen a student care so little about fitting in.

It was as if he **wanted** to be left out.

And, sure enough, he was.

By the end of the week, Hiro Sakurai had systematically frozen himself out of every clique in the whole school.

Even the **losers** wanted nothing to do with him.

The girls at lunch quickly reached a consensus on Hiro...

What a disappointment.

Yeah, a real letdown.

And not **nearly** as hot as Keiko said he was.

...then stopped discussing him altogether.

So did I. But that doesn't mean I stopped **thinking** about him.

I found myself recalling the look on Hiro's face when I startled him out in the rice paddy.

It was as if I'd inadvertently broken through the wall he always kept between himself and others.

That look in his eyes-- before they hardened and grew cold--

--that look told me there was more to Hiro than what he allowed people to see.

There was something hidden behind those eyes. Something no one knew about.

There was another thing. What was he doing out there in the rice paddy that day?

What was that thing he'd been holding in his hands...

...the thing he was so anxious to keep me from seeing?

The Miki of junior year would never have allowed herself to become obsessed with someone else's secrets.

She was far too sensible and well behaved to do something like that.

She'd have minded her own business and stayed where she belonged.

The Miki of senior year, on the other hand...

...came up with a plan.

A gift basket.

For Hiro Sakurai.

You are completely out of your mind.

Look, I can tell he's actually a nice guy.

He just needs a chance--away from school--to get to know some people.

So we make a gift basket, go to his front door, ring the bell, and...

...you're gonna see a different side of him. I promise.

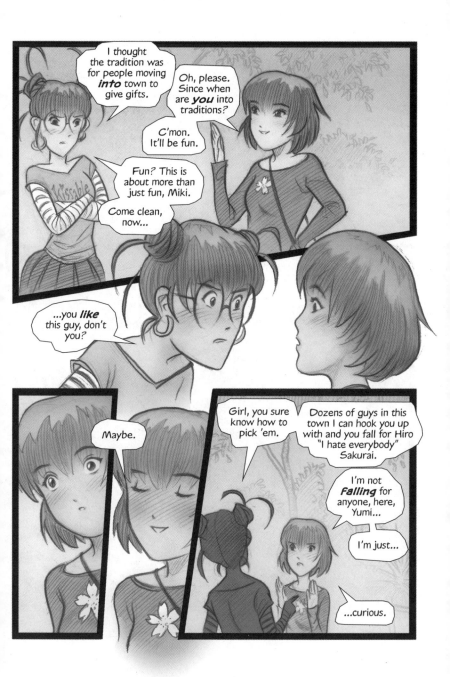

37

So am I, actually.

Do I get to be there when you give it to him?

You kidding? I'm gonna need you with me on this one, Yumi, start to finish.

All right, I'm in.

And so began Operation Gift Basket...

We went to all the best stores in Fukuyama...

We're shopping for **Hiro**, not you!

...and debated the merits of every item before making any final purchases.

Would he eat hazelnut truffles?

No way. With guys it's strictly beef jerky.

ヘイゼルナッツ
トリュフ
¥1000

And after a minor meltdown over which card to buy...

Tasteful flowers!

Beach babe!

...we had everything we needed for a **very** generous gift basket.

I spent a whole evening arranging the different items, making sure everything was just right.

It looked pretty fabulous, if I do say so myself.

The next day Yumi and I went to Hiro's house right after school.

It was a strange place--the only European-style building in town--and its haunted-house look just added to my nervousness.

How would Hiro react? Would he be pleased? Grateful?

More importantly, would he do what I wanted him to do: invite us in...

...and reveal a little more about who he was?

I hope he likes it.

Likes it? After all this, he'd better give you a big wet kiss on the lips!

43

45

On the second Saturday in April, when my friends and I were having a picnic up at Fukuyama Castle...

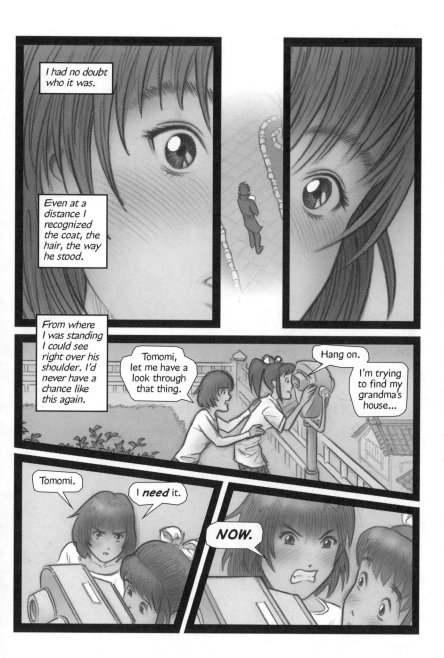

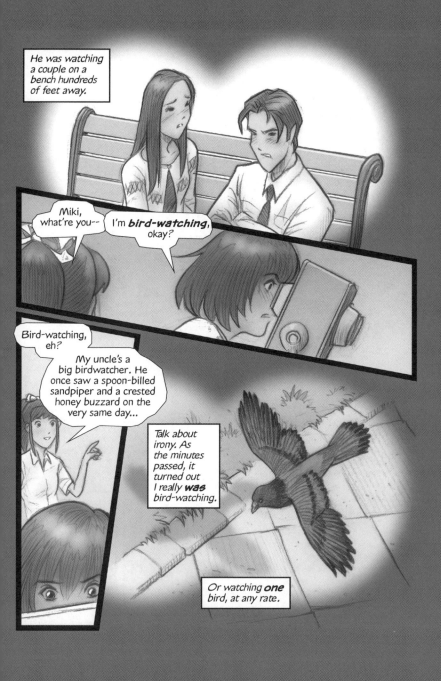

He was watching a couple on a bench hundreds of feet away.

Miki, what're you--

I'm **bird-watching**, okay?

Bird-watching, eh?

My uncle's a big birdwatcher. He once saw a spoon-billed sandpiper and a crested honey buzzard on the very same day...

Talk about irony. As the minutes passed, it turned out I really **was** bird-watching.

Or watching **one** bird, at any rate.

A dark-gray pigeon kept flying back and forth between Hiro and the couple.

It spent most of its time near the couple, but periodically flew to Hiro for brief visits.

Soon it was clear that the pigeon **belonged** to Hiro.

He was its master, able to have it come and go as he pleased.

Me, I can't stand birds. They freak me out.

Especially the eyes...

I was so intent on following the movements of the pigeon I almost missed it when the couple--who had been having a big argument--abruptly split up.

The woman marched off in a huff...

...and the man left soon afterward.

Then Hiro closed his notebook, tucked it into his coat, and walked away.

The pigeon flapped up to a telephone wire, becoming indistinguishable from any other bird.

And, within seconds...

...there was nothing left to see.

There was no turning back.

I couldn't walk away from all this stuff as if it were no big deal.

So I made a decision.

It was time to get to know Hiro Sakurai--

--get to **really** know him--

--once and for all.

64

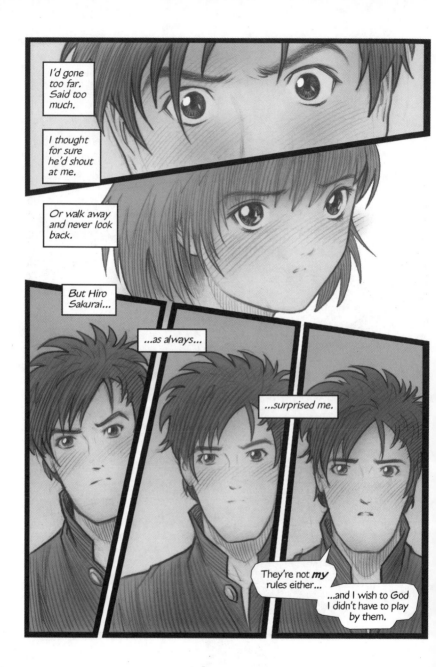

I'd gone too far. Said too much.

I thought for sure he'd shout at me.

Or walk away and never look back.

But Hiro Sakurai...

...as always...

...surprised me.

They're not *my* rules either...

...and I wish to God I didn't have to play by them.

And that's all it took.

From that moment on there was an understanding between Hiro and me.

I would become the closest thing to a friend he'd allow himself to have...

...so long as I respected his privacy.

Not exactly what I'd been hoping for.

But it was a start.

As the days went by and April rolled into May, Hiro began to loosen up around me.

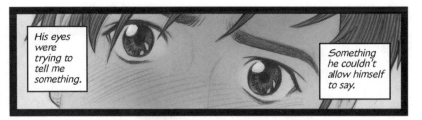

His eyes were trying to tell me something.

Something he couldn't allow himself to say.

Sure, Hiro.

I'll go somewhere with you.

Hiro took me through some fields behind the school to a stone stairway, hundreds of steps from top to bottom.

It led to a secluded shrine high in the hills above Fukuyama. I'd been there before and said so to Hiro.

"That's not where we're going," he replied.

Sure enough, Hiro led me straight past the shrine to a steep footpath behind it, one that led farther up into the hills.

The trail quickly became as rough as the woods surrounding it. There were no steps other than some tangled tree roots and the occasional mossy boulder or two.

Soon I began to think Hiro had no idea where we were going...

...and that the whole thing would turn out to be a huge waste of time.

Of course...

That he was a good person. A warm person. And someone who needed a friend.

Needed one pretty desperately, from what I could see.

I kept my questions to myself.

For now it was enough to know that Hiro was trying--

--in his own strange, cautious way--

--to make a place for me in his life.

Hiro and I began to spend more time together. As much as he could spare, anyway.

He said he had a "part-time job" that kept him very busy.

"A job involving notebooks and pigeons," I thought. But that topic, I knew, was strictly off-limits.

One evening after kyuudou practice Hiro offered to walk me home.

It couldn't hurt to ask just **one** question, could it?

Hiro, I've been wondering about something.

Yeah?

FFSWIT!

Hiro led me to his house. There, he said, I could wash up and borrow some dry clothes from his mother.

Nearly getting hit by a car is not something I would normally think of as a stroke of good luck...

...but under the circumstances I felt as if I'd just won the lottery.

Hiro Sakurai--the guy who wouldn't let me so much as peek into his locker at school--was inviting me to go inside his house!

Still, as we neared the front door, I could see Hiro was having second thoughts.

That this might be one broken rule too many.

Are you sure about this, Hiro?

My house isn't so far from here. And it's not *that* cold out...

No.

I mean, **yes**: I'm sure.

I've **got** to do this for you. You're soaking wet, and...

...and...

...and it's not a big deal, right?

I'm only...

...doing...

...what any normal human being would do in this situation.

Weird: He was going to such lengths to justify all this to me...

...but I knew the person he was **really** trying to persuade...

Right?

...was himself.

Without another word he opened the door...

...and I stepped inside...

...past one of the last lines dividing Hiro's world from my own.

Hiro introduced me to his mother.

She looked at me as if I were an apparition.

Clearly this was the very first time Hiro had allowed anyone into the house...

...or any other house they'd ever lived in.

She exchanged wary glances with Hiro...

...then tried to act casual...

...turning to show me where I could wash up and change.

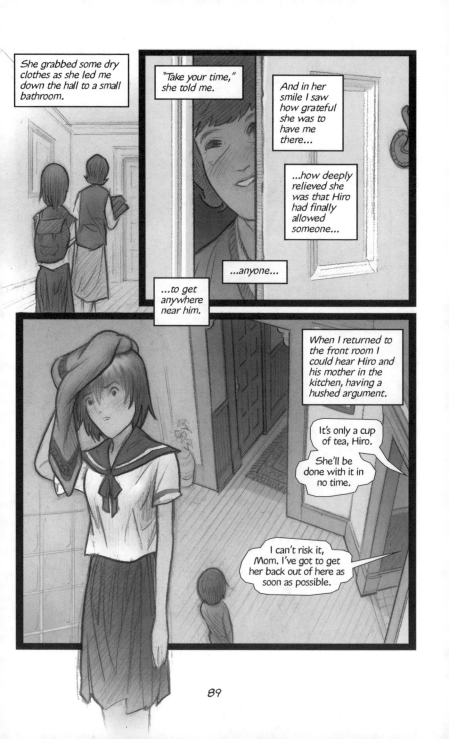

I crept over to get a closer look.

Behind the door was a stairway leading down to the basement...

...and at the bottom of the stairs...

Hiro helped me into a jacket and hustled me out the front door.

We walked the rest of the way to my house in total silence.

I kept sneaking glances at Hiro...

...trying to guess his thoughts...

...or just read any sort of emotion in his eyes...

...but his face had turned to stone.

The Hiro I'd worked so hard to get to know had completely shut himself down...

...and run off to hide inside the solitude of his own mind.

"This won't last," I told myself.

"Tomorrow everything will go back to normal."

That night as I lay in bed I tried to visualize what I'd seen in Hiro's basement.

What was it?

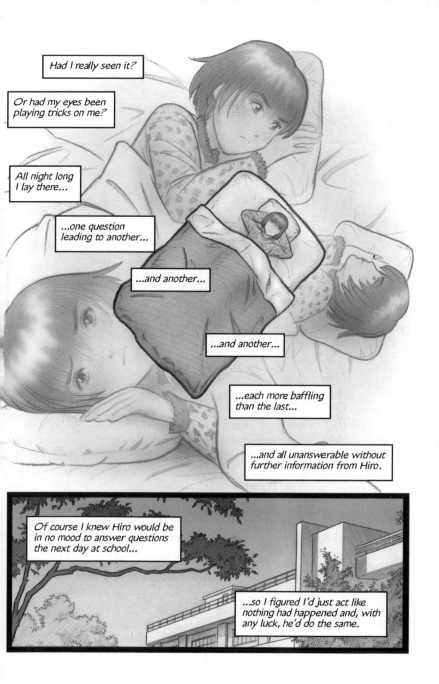

Had I really seen it?

Or had my eyes been playing tricks on me?

All night long I lay there...

...one question leading to another...

...and another...

...and another...

...each more baffling than the last...

...and all unanswerable without further information from Hiro.

Of course I knew Hiro would be in no mood to answer questions the next day at school...

...so I figured I'd just act like nothing had happened and, with any luck, he'd do the same.

97

98

The roof.

Kids only went up there when they had **really** big news to share.

Was Hiro about to let me in on one of his big secrets?

"Don't pry," I told myself.

"Just let him open up at his own pace."

When we got to the roof, Hiro led me straight across to a guardrail overlooking the kyuudou range.

100

103

105

107

For the rest of the week I was adrift.

I shuffled through the usual routines, enjoying nothing, like an uninterested spectator watching her own life crawl by.

True to his word, Hiro completely banished me from his world.

Even when our paths crossed--

--and Hiro saw to it that such occurrences were exceedingly rare--

--he blew by me as if I weren't even there.

So I did what any sensible girl would do. I invited Yumi to meet me at our favorite café for an afternoon snack...

...and just totally poured my heart out to her.

...and that was it. He said good-bye and hasn't given me the time of day since.

Miki, take it from me: All boys are heartbreakers in the end, but this guy is, like, off the charts.

You should be breathing a sigh of relief to have finally gotten rid of him.

I mean, stand back and look at what you had there.

A guy who treated you badly.

A guy who was hiding stuff from you all the time.

A guy who you saw--with your own eyes--spying on people.

Okay, so **you** were spying on **him** at the time, but still...

I know, Yumi, I know.

110

What is Hiro's so-called "part-time job"?

What is it that's standing between us?

I've got a right to know this stuff.

He can't chase me out of his life for no reason at all.

He owes me an explanation.

And since he's decided not to *give* me any explanation...

...I'll just have to get one on my own.

...okay, that settles it!

Tomomi will do "Namida No Lonely Night" and Keiko will do "Love Is Ichiban."

Mi-chan, it's almost your turn again.

You know what you're gonna do?

Oh yeah.

I know *exactly* what I'm going to do.

The next afternoon I followed Hiro as he left the school and headed into town.

I kept my distance, making sure he wouldn't see me.

I ended up following him all over Fukuyama, watching his every move.

In the space of an hour he went to four different locations.

An apartment building. A farmhouse. A shop. A restaurant.

At each place he took notes.

Sometimes I saw the pigeon.

Sometimes I didn't.

114

Following Hiro soon became a habit.

I began doing it every day, with every spare minute I had.

Before long I knew the places that were on his rounds, and the locations that demanded more of his attention than others.

One time Hiro nearly caught me in the act.

I was faced with a stark choice.

Either stop spying...

115

...or start **really** spying.

So these are the most powerful ones you've got?

Oh yeah. With those you'll be able to see clear across town.

And so I continued watching Hiro from a distance, trying-- and failing--to get a handle on what he was up to.

I knew he was monitoring the activities of certain people around town...

...but I couldn't see what they had in common.

And as for what Hiro was **doing** with all this information...

...well, that was entirely beyond me.

116

One night I lingered in the spot where my Hiro-watching always came to an end...

...beside a window, half buried in weeds, at the back of Hiro's house.

It allowed a tantalizing glimpse of the basement...

...but little more than an area of the floor about ten foot square.

Occasionally I could see Hiro's shadow or his feet as he crossed to the stairs, but that was it.

But there was no shaking the idea once it had occurred to me.

I knew I could spend the rest of my life following Hiro around Fukuyama...

...and still not learn what I'd uncover in a thirty-second tour of that basement.

NNNNGH

I tried all the doors and windows: locked, naturally.

Then, just when I had nearly talked myself into putting a stone through a window, I found the very thing I needed.

A storm door. Leading straight into the basement.

It was chained shut with a lock the size of my fist.

But the hinges were rusting...

...and the wood beneath them had started to rot.

But there was no turning back.

I realized now that my every move over the last days and weeks had brought me to this place...

...and that I could no more turn away at this point than cease to breathe, or command my heart to stop beating.

I moved the unhinged door aside and stepped down into the darkness.

When I reached the basement floor, I found a lamp hanging from the ceiling.

I took hold of the cord and switched it on.

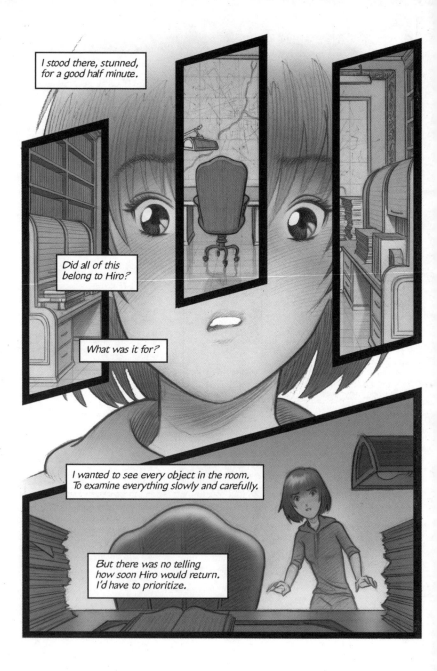

I stood there, stunned, for a good half minute.

Did all of this belong to Hiro?

What was it for?

I wanted to see every object in the room. To examine everything slowly and carefully.

But there was no telling how soon Hiro would return. I'd have to prioritize.

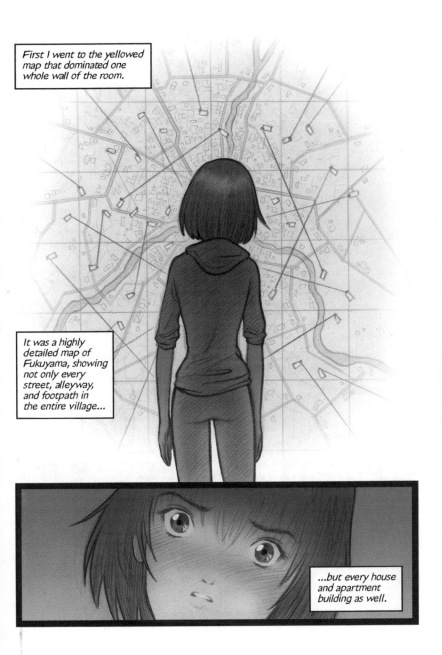

First I went to the yellowed map that dominated one whole wall of the room.

It was a highly detailed map of Fukuyama, showing not only every street, alleyway, and footpath in the entire village...

...but every house and apartment building as well.

125

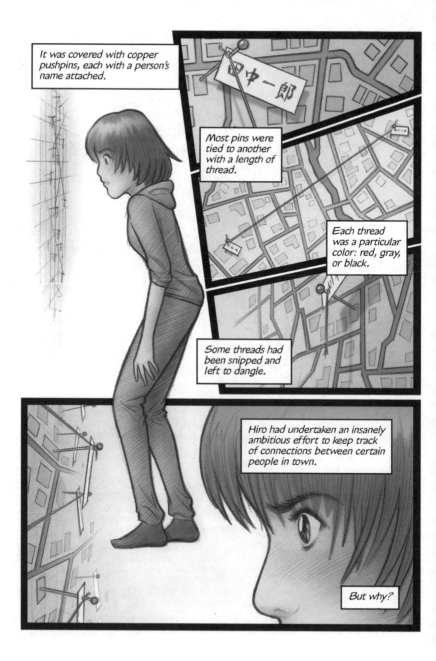

It was covered with copper pushpins, each with a person's name attached.

Most pins were tied to another with a length of thread.

Each thread was a particular color: red, gray, or black.

Some threads had been snipped and left to dangle.

Hiro had undertaken an insanely ambitious effort to keep track of connections between certain people in town.

But why?

126

I turned my attention to the bookshelves that lined the walls.

It was like a library consisting of only one type of book.

There were hundreds upon hundreds of them, each precisely the same height and thickness.

I pulled one down and began reading at random.

"Mr. Matsu moto has not yet noticed Miss Hayashi," went a typical passage, "but it is no wonder: He is still wasting too much time in the vain pursuit of Miss Yamada."

"It is still far too soon," the writer concluded, "to arrange a chance meeting."

They were notations in a hardbound notebook just like Hiro's, but the handwriting wasn't his.

Indeed, this entry was dated June 3rd, 1903. The book had surely passed through several generations before coming into Hiro's possession.

I began pulling books down by the armful, sampling as many of them as I could.

128

And with all this talk of arranging "chance meetings"...

...clearly these people were doing far more than just watching and taking notes.

I reshelved the books and crossed to Hiro's desk.

There were stacks of books and papers, charts and graphs...

...ample evidence that at any given time Hiro was dealing with vast amounts of information...

...relating to hundreds of people.

The entry continued: "I believe Manami is ready for a brief glance from Yohei Chiba..."

"...which could be arranged as early as next Friday."

"As for a first conversation, I would estimate two more weeks at least, and perhaps as many as--"

KCHUK

The door.

Hiro!

135

136

After several minutes I worked up the courage to speak.

I'm sorry, Hiro.

I don't expect you to forgive me for what I've done...

...but I want you to at least hear the words.

And...

...I really have no idea what you're part of here, but...

...whoever your superiors are, this is still just between you and me now, right?

They don't know anything yet.

His silence told me it was true.

So why don't you explain some of this to me...

...and see if we can't come up with a plan?

Together.

138

Hiro remained silent, but I could see a decision forming on his face.

Breaking things off with me had been all about keeping me away from this room.

Now that I was already here, the reasoning behind all the evasions and secretiveness had suddenly evaporated.

"Why not?" I could almost hear him say.

"Why not tell her..."

"...why not tell her everything?"

Hiro asked me to sit down.

Does all of this...

...make sense to you?

I opened my mouth but no words came.

Part of me wanted Hiro to laugh and say it was all an elaborate prank.

But I knew Hiro meant everything he'd said. Meant it with all his heart.

So there were really only two possibilities.

Either Hiro was describing the world as it actually was...

...or else he was completely out of his mind.

143

Finally I managed a simple question.

Are you telling me that... ...you're not human?

Not anymore, no.

When I became a Deliverer several years ago...

...I was transformed into a quasi-celestial being.

Since that time I have had no need for sleep or food or even air.

I cannot be killed...

...which is not to say that I will live forever.

Like all Deliverers, I will die when Mother Freya--

--the Goddess of Love--

--decides that my work is finished.

Only that the hour of my death is preordained.

My heart was pounding.

Hiro really *was* crazy.

There was no other reasonable explanation.

He had somehow deluded himself into believing all this...

...and now he was asking me to join him in his madness.

145

Then he lifted his hands, palms up, before his face...

...and a tiny glowing sphere appeared.

It grew larger...

...and larger...

...and...

...out of thin air...

...a creature came into being...

...right before my very eyes.

Anra is a Hold Spirit.

Every Deliverer is paired with one.

Anra jumped onto my lap like an affectionate cat.

She weighed so little it was as if she were made of paper.

It's Anra that draws dying love from one couple and holds it...

...until it can be delivered to another.

But that is only the beginning of her abilities.

Look into her eyes, Miki.

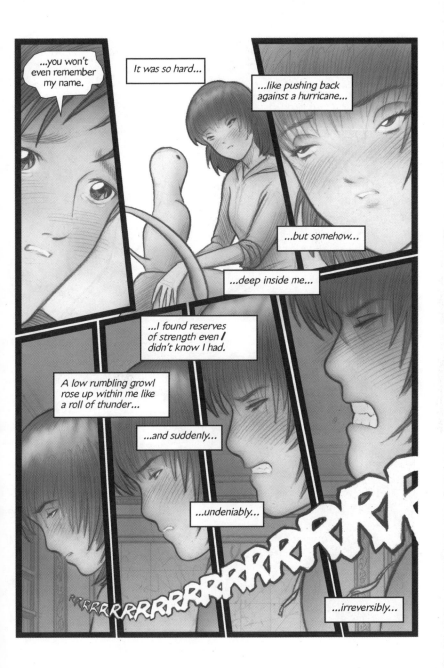

152

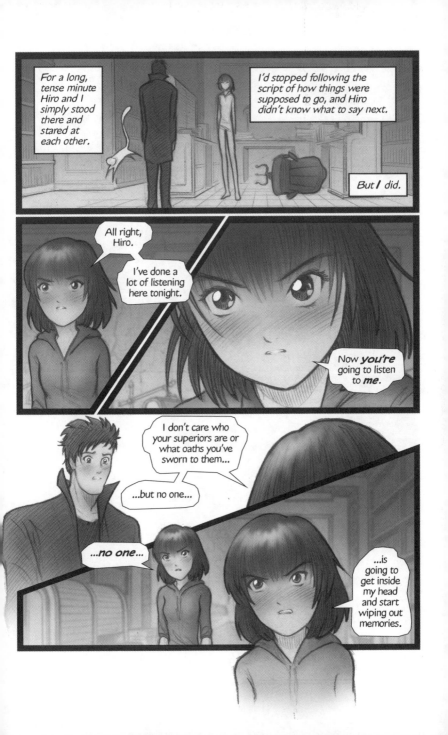

Least of all memories of you.

Miki...

I'm not finished.

Now, you may believe you're...

...half-celestial or whatever it is you call yourself.

But I know in my heart that part of you is still human.

Very human.

Whether you want to face up to it or not, *that* part of you...

...wants me around.

155

You don't understand, Miki.

I took a **sacred oath**.

Nothing is more sacred than your right to be with whomever you choose.

And anyone who tells you otherwise...

...is no more superior to you than a mosquito.

Look, Hiro...

...you've spent a lot of time looking at other people's lives...

...and not enough looking at your own.

Well, I'm looking at your life right now...

...and here's what I see.

157

Hiro walked me home that night, my memories intact.

And though I didn't get everything I wanted--

--a closer look at some of those notebooks would have been nice--

--I got what most mattered to me: an end to Hiro's ignoring me at school, and, even better...

...the beginning of a much deeper friendship than we'd had before.

And friendship, Hiro made clear, was exactly where things would stay.

It was absolutely forbidden, by order of Mother Freya herself...

...for Deliverers to fall in love with human beings.

Not my ideal state of affairs.

But hey...

...who was I to defy the Goddess of Love?

...just because.

To the real Miki,
for whom I fall a little more
every day

First published in the United States by HarperTeen, an imprint of HarperCollins *Publishers*, 2007

First published in paperback in Great Britain by HarperCollins *Children's Books* 2008
HarperCollins *Children's Books* is a division of HarperCollins *Publishers* Ltd
77-85 Fulham Palace Road, Hammersmith, London W6 8JB

The HarperCollins *Children's Books* website address is
www.harpercollinschildrensbooks.co.uk

/

Copyright © Mark Crilley 2007

Mark Crilley asserts the moral right to be identified as the author and illustrator of this work

ISBN-13 978-0-00-724660-1
ISBN-10 0-00-724660-9

Printed and bound in the UK by Martins the Printers

Has Miki fallen too hard?
Keep reading to find out more!

Turn the page for a preview of

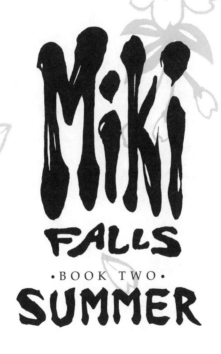

Miki

FALLS

· BOOK TWO ·

SUMMER

And I don't mean that in a poetic sense.

I mean *saw* it.

With my own eyes.

The trick is to keep a good distance.

Any closer than this and people know they're being followed.

Hiro had been monitoring the couple for more than nine weeks.

Though he had never met either of them, he knew them intimately...

...for he had studied them with great care...

...keeping detailed records of how they treated each other...

...how they spoke to each other...

...even how they handled objects belonging to the other.

6

...providing him with crucial information about the weakening love that yet remained between Kanchi and Risa.

So how does one get a total stranger to drop a bowl of shaved ice?

Well, turns out that if you happen to be a firefly...

...it's surprisingly easy.

FZIT

KYAAAA!

Could this be the season for love?

Now that Miki knows Hiro's secret, maybe they can be together at last. But knowledge, like love, can be a very dangerous thing.

The more Hiro falls for Miki, the more he wants to protect her. Will love force them apart?

HarperCollins *Children's Books*